Back to the Beginning

Book 8 in the Coach's Boys Series

Kristy K. James

A COACH'S BOYS SPECIAL EDITION

During their regular bi-monthly 'guy's night out,' an ill-timed phone call brings back memories of the year Ed first came into their lives. A year that brought painful changes, unbearable heartache, and fear over what the future might bring.

In this installment of the Coach's Boys series, you'll catch up with what's going on in the lives of Dan, Sam, Chris, Jon, Cal, and Ed. You'll also get to know who they were twenty years ago – and the challenges they faced that helped them become the men they are today.

Connect with Kristy...

http://kristykjames.net/
https://www.facebook.com/kristykjames
Be sure to follow Kristy on Bookbub to get notifications for her new releases!
https://www.bookbub.com/authors/kristy-k-james

Other Works by Kristy K. James

Coach's Boys Series

The Daddy Pact, Book 1[1]

A Hero for Holly, Book 2[2]

A Harry Situation, Book 3[3]

Her Best Friend Jon, Book 4[4]

Code Red Christmas, Book 5[5]

Darby's Dilemma, Book 6[6]

The Detective's Second Chance, Book 7[7]

Back to the Beginning, Book 8[8]

Holding Out For Love, Coach's Boys Companion Story[9] (*should be read between books 6 & 7*)

---

1. http://kristykjames.net/books/the-daddy-pact/

2. http://kristykjames.net/books/a-hero-for-holly/

3. http://kristykjames.net/books/a-harry-situation/

4. http://kristykjames.net/books/her-best-friend-jon/

5. http://kristykjames.net/books/code-red-christmas/

6. http://kristykjames.net/books/darbys-dilemma/

7. http://kristykjames.net/books/the-detectives-second-chance/

8. http://kristykjames.net/books/10327/

9. http://kristykjames.net/books/holding-out-for-love/

Cooking With the Coach's Boys[10]

---

10. http://kristykjames.net/books/
cooking-with-the-coachs-boys-hometown-recipes-from-the-whole-gang-2/

A Royal Sweethearts Romance Novel Series

The Casteloria Royals

---

1. http://kristykjames.net/books/a-prince-on-the-run/

2. http://kristykjames.net/books/a-cool-summer-in-paradise/

3. http://kristykjames.net/books/a-cold-day-in-paradise/

Hemisphere/Paranormal Romance

The Ripple[1]

---

1. http://kristykjames.net/books/the-ripple/

Haunted Depot: The Ghost Curse Series

The Secret, Book 1[1]
The Depot, Book 2[2]
A Merry Depot Christmas, Book 3[3]

---

1. http://kristykjames.net/books/the-depot/

2. http://kristykjames.net/books/the-depot/

3. http://kristykjames.net/books/a-merry-depot-christmas/

Special Wishes Time Travel Romance

His Only Love[1]
Her Long Road Home[2]

---

1. http://kristykjames.net/books/holding-on-to-yesterday/

2. http://kristykjames.net/books/the-accidental-wish/

Other Fiction:

Enza[1]
Josh[2]
The Secret Admirer[3]
Erin's Christmas Wish[4]
A Fine Mess[5]
Reluctant Guardian[6]

---

1. http://kristykjames.net/books/enza/

2. http://kristykjames.net/books/josh/

3. http://kristykjames.net/books/the-secret-admirer/

4. http://kristykjames.net/books/erins-christmas-wish/

5. http://kristykjames.net/books/a-fine-mess/

6. http://kristykjames.net/books/reluctant-guardian/

Kathie... What can I say? You did it again. You not only found the most clunky scene I've ever written – then helped me to smooth out its edges so readers won't beat their heads against the wall trying to figure out what I 'meant to say,' you spotted the typos I never seem to see. Thank you, thank you, thank you! :)

~~~Present Day~~~

Ed Winslow sat behind the desk that had been his for the past twenty years. Added to being a street cop for eight years before the promotion, he was a couple of years shy of the requisite thirty. But he'd put in so much overtime after Teresa took the girls, the department offered him an early retirement package.

And he was glad because he'd had enough. He was tired of trying to fight crime in a world that had changed too much over three decades. Yeah. Past time to move on to the proverbial greener pastures.

Like his new little hole in the wall office in Charlotte. Located above a used bookstore, it came complete with a flight of stairs only those of a robust constitution, or an extreme case of desperation, would want to tackle.

It put him in mind of all the shows he'd watched as a kid. Orange-ish brick walls, faded wooden floors, and tall, narrow windows overlooking the main street below. Jenna insisted on buying some throw rugs to add a little color and helped him choose new office furnishings. In his mind, it was perfect for the new chapter in his life.

Ed Winslow, Private Detective

He smiled just a hint of a smile and glanced out the wall of glass to the outer office, fondly known as The Asylum—because that's where they all slowly lost their minds.

Too many rules and regulations made it hard to do the job now. Too many loopholes and excuses allowed too many criminals to walk away instead of doing the time they deserved. All it did was make for more paperwork and headaches for everyone.

Yeah. He was done.

The party, to wish him well before he walked out of the department for the last time tonight, was still going strong as eight o'clock came and went. But Ed wasn't in much of a mood to celebrate.

Somehow, he thought he'd feel jubilant when this day came. Instead, he felt a little melancholy. Glad as he would be to stop making the daily commute and having to deal with society's criminals, he would miss it a little too. This job had kept him from losing his mind on more than one occasion.

He didn't often allow himself to dwell on the past but sometimes, the memories needed pulling out and tonight, they needed to be remembered...

1997...

She lied.

She lied and like a fool, he'd believed her. Now the girls were gone and there wasn't a thing he could do about it. Nothing that didn't involve a capital offense and a twenty to life prison sentence anyway.

Not that he hadn't been tempted to say the heck with it many times over the past six months. But the fact that he wouldn't fare well in an enclosed space with cop-hating inmates kept him from hunting his ex-wife down like a rabid animal.

A week ago, Mark Conroy—his boss and former foster father—sat him down for a heart-to-heart. Grief and anger were affecting Ed's job performance and he was worried. Inability to focus in certain situations had gotten many officers hurt or killed. And not just them but their partners too.

No one blamed him. Life, in the form of a manipulative ex, had dealt him a bad, heart breaking hand. But Ed needed to face facts. Mary and Annie were gone. Much as it hurt, there was nothing he could do about it now. It was time to stop living in the past and move forward with his life as best he could.

On one hand, he knew Mark was right. On the other- It was so hard to let them go.

Two nights ago, he'd finally decided to take the advice. To stop tearing himself up with memories of what he should have done, what he could have done, and what he hadn't done.

After hunting up a dozen boxes, he'd started packing. All of the clothes and toys he'd kept at the apartment for them. All of their cartoon character bedding. All of their books. Everything that reminded him of them would have to go.

Except the pictures. For those, he'd rented a safe deposit box at his bank. Once a year, he'd allow himself to get them, spend one day making himself miserable remembering, and then he'd take them back. Of course, he'd had to keep one out. Just one of them sitting on Mary's bed, dressed in frilly princess nightgowns, freshly scrubbed and ready to visit dreamland. That one, he'd had laminated and tucked it behind his driver's license.

Yesterday, after dismantling the beds and hauling all of the furniture out to the living room, he called the charity. If they could send someone, he had a truckload of children's stuff, all in good condition. They could have it.

This morning though, he broke down and went through the boxes, pulling out Mary's favorite Christmas storybook, something he'd read to her a hundred times or more, along with the doll Annie couldn't sleep without when he had them for his weekends. Those, he couldn't part with either.

The rest?

It was all he could do to keep from throwing the boxes into the truck they'd sent, along with a frail senior citizen driver who couldn't help with most of it. Bad enough he'd had to pack it all up, now he had to literally give it away. It hurt more than he'd ever be able to express. It made him angrier than he'd ever been in his life. And it made him want to hit his knees and sob until the hurt went away.

Except it would never go away. Never.

An hour later, he watched as the old box truck rattled down the road filled to almost overflowing with all of their things. Maybe now he could keep his daughters safely in a part of his heart where they couldn't torture him every second of every day.

With a sigh, he walked back into his now emptier apartment, determined to focus on the future. Instead, he heard the echoes of happier times. Little girl voices chattering from the moment they woke up until they fell asleep at night, exhausted from their busy days. Delighted peals of laughter as they chased each other up and down the halls. Their soft, "I love you, Daddy's," as they cuddled in his lap.

Shaking the memories away, he closed and locked the door, then sat down in his recliner.

What was done was done. There was no going back. No second chances. No matter how much he might wish he could change what had happened, that somehow, he could be given a do-over, he'd been stupid enough to believe the pack of lies he'd been fed. The game was finished. Teresa had won.

He'd read somewhere that a man his age had a life expectancy of seventy-four-point-four years. That meant he only had forty-nine left to fill. To find enough things to keep him so busy he could forget the past seven years. At least part of the time. If he couldn't, he didn't know how he'd survive the next five decades.

During their talk, Mark had a list of suggestions as long as his arm of things Ed could do. From volunteering at a local soup kitchen to taking some courses at the community college.

While he didn't mind donating cash to charities, he wasn't much into the giving of his time right now. Not because the ones he supported weren't worthy causes but because the last thing he needed right now was to see other people going through rough times too. He felt so bad for himself he didn't know if he could find any compassion for others. Not right now.

There was one thing though...

A little league coaching position that had opened up out in Charlotte. The guy who had been doing it had been transferred and they needed a replacement ASAP. He liked baseball. Softball was close enough. And working with a bunch of rowdy teenage boys was bound to be a good distraction. Totally different from what he was used to with the girls-

No. He was done thinking about that part of his life. It was over, time to move on.

Maybe he'd take the job, the unpaid job, and make Mark happy. He might not be the best coach on the planet but he sure had enough spare time and, from what Mark told him, he couldn't do any worse than the other guy had. The team was last in their league.

~~~**Present day**~~~

"You know," Jon Rambo said, tossing a brightly colored reverse card onto the pile in the middle of the table, "there was a time when we'd have been playing poker and drinking something a little stronger than colas."

Ed rolled his eyes. Except for the occasional glass of wine with a fancy dinner, neither he nor the guys had ever been much for drinking *stronger* stuff. They had, however, played plenty of poker—for pennies, dimes, nickels, and quarters for the really good hands.

Not much anymore though. One by one, as they'd become domesticated husbands and fathers, even their taste in entertainment had changed to a more family friendly kind.

"Yes!" Dan Mulholland said, a grinchy grin curving his lips as he threw a draw four card on top. "Red. Gotcha!" Jon scowled, but pulled four new cards from the top of the deck without complaint. "We're all dads now. The day you and Hannah became parents, your days of being footloose and fancy free ended. Oh wait! You never were footloose and fancy free, were you?" Everyone chuckled, even Jon because he knew he used to lead a very narrow, dull life.

"And I, for one, couldn't be happier about that," Ed, the proud grandfather of four month old Nicky, declared, just before he announced, "Whew. Thought one of you would have caught me when I forgot to tell you I only had one card left last time, but you didn't. I win." Jon scowled again, looking at the dozen or so cards in his hand. From his expression, it appeared he'd drawn at least a few that would hurt his already sorry score.

The girls were at Cal and Darby's making Christmas decorations with the kids while the guys were spending their night out at Dan and

16

Jess's. It was a tradition that never lost its appeal no matter which bunch had the kids. Their wives just tended to plan projects while they were content popping a bunch of corn and watching movies or ordering pizzas and playing video games.

Tonight, all of the kids—except for Nicky—would be helping, even the triplets, who would be two in a couple of months. Ed couldn't help it. He was always a little jealous of the girls when they had the kids. He looked on all of them as his grandkids but to be a grandfather to his youngest daughter's child? That was something he'd never believed would happen. But it had and even though he got to spend more time with them now that he'd retired and was working for himself, he'd never tire of holding that baby.

As Sam was dealing the next hand, Jon's cell phone rang. Judging by the expression on his face, they all knew who it was.

"Yeah. I'll be right there," Jon said, after listening for about thirty seconds. His voice was as toneless as a robot when he ended the call and got up from the table. "I have to cut out of here for a while. There's a furnace that needs fixing." He walked to the foyer, Dan hot on his heels. "I shouldn't be gone too long."

"I don't know why he doesn't just tell them to eat dirt," Cal muttered when the front door closed behind him and Dan returned to the table. "Every time they call, he about breaks his neck to get over there help them. It's like they have some hold over him."

"They do," Ed said softly, unable to hide the frustration he felt over the situation. "They're his parents. He's trying to prove that no matter how much they hurt and neglected him, he's the better person."

"Still, after everything they did to him—" Cal shook his head.

"At least he had you guys," Ed pointed out, though he agreed with the other guys. Jon had done far more than he should have for his abusive parents and no one would blame him if he finally said enough.

"He didn't have me," Chris reminded him, grabbing a potato chip from the paper plate beside his cards. Though he was Jon's business partner in C&J Construction, he hadn't met any of the guys until they'd started college.

"True enough, but he did have the rest." Ed couldn't imagine a young Jon surviving his childhood without his friends.

"He had you too," Dan said quietly. "I think we all helped keep him from doing something stupid but I don't know if we'd have been enough as we got older. There was something about you though. I don't know where Jon would be today if you hadn't started coaching our team. The summer we met you was one of the worst ever for him."

"It sure was," Cal muttered, his jaws clenched.

And it had been, Ed knew, for all of them, but especially for Jon *and* Cal.

"That was the summer you were dating that girl, Sam." Dan's brows drew together as he tried to remember her name.

"Deirdre," Sam said, not surprised the name still tasted sour on his tongue. "Her name was Deirdre and I was tutoring her, not dating her."

That girl nearly scarred him for life. Well, maybe it hadn't been that dramatic but she'd certainly scared him off girls for a long time. He hadn't dated much before he met Holly and it was because he'd always wondered whether a woman liked him for him or because of what he could do for her. Especially after he'd started making C&J Construction rich with his one of a kind house designs.

Yeah. That had all been courtesy of Deirdre Hollister.

She'd been nearly three years older than him but he'd been tall for his age, and more mature than most boys in high school. He'd been crushing on her for most of the school year and the day he'd found her crying in the park, head bent down, her slender shoulders shaking as she'd wept, had nearly broken his heart...

1997...

"You're Sam Jensen, aren't you," she sniffed, wiping the tears from her cheeks with her fingers and trying to smile. When she pointed at the empty space on the bench, right next to her, Sam could hardly breathe.

"Uh- Yeah. Yes. I'm him," he managed to stammer, sitting on the very edge of the bench. He couldn't have been more stunned that the most beautiful girl in school was talking to him. That she knew his name. "Are—are you all right?" Of course she wasn't all right, she was crying for heaven's sake. He wanted to kick himself for asking.

"No." The whisper was punctuated with another fat tear rolling down her cheek. "I'm so stupid!"

"You're not stupid at all," he assured her, wishing he had even a little experience with girls. Dan would be able to tell him what to do. If Dan was here, but he wasn't. Nope. He was going to have to wing it and the thought gave him chills. Not the good kind either.

"I am. I wish I was smart like you are. I'm probably going to flunk and everyone I know is going to get to go to ninth grade and I'm just going to be stuck in eighth again." She began to sob again, her shoulders shaking, and she leaned her head against his shoulder. Sam could hardly breathe when she told him her only hope was summer school but she was afraid she'd fail that too.

By that point, he was ready to do anything to make her happy again and so he offered to tutor her until she understood basic algebra, something he'd aced by the time he'd entered third grade. Before she left for home, they agreed to meet twice a week at the local library. Deirdre's dazzling smile rivaled the bright spring sunshine and she threw her arms around his shoulders, hugging him tight for what felt like forever. She stepped away before he thought to hug her back.

Sam carried the memory of that hug with him for days. When he saw her on the library steps, he prayed for a repeat but she just smiled at him, walking by his side as they went to find a table.

"I really appreciate this, Sam," Deirdre said two weeks later, her voice soft as silk as she reached across the table in a quiet alcove to squeeze his hand. "I don't know what I'd do if you weren't helping me. Look at this! The teacher thought I'd cheated—until I told him you were working with me."

She handed him a test paper with a C minus which, she said, was a big improvement over the red F's she'd been getting, but they still had some work to do.

"That's really good," he told her, a smile turning the corners of his lips up.

"Thanks! My parents are so happy they said once I start getting all B's, they want you to come over for supper so they can meet you and thank you in person."

Sam swallowed hard. Supper? This was major! When a girl's parents wanted to meet a guy, that meant something. He wasn't sure what, exactly, but he knew it was a good thing.

For a moment, he had visions of walking into school on the first day of class, his arm wrapped around Deirdre, her head resting on his shoulder. And then he gave himself a mental shake, banished the vision, and focused on the task at hand.

They had work to do if his dreams were going to come true. And he knew they would because she'd started kissing him on the cheek at the end of each session. If they didn't get her homework done, he'd never get a real kiss. A kiss where her lips were pressed against his.

HE NEVER HAD GOTTEN that kiss. He used to think she was the sweetest, most beautiful girl in the world. Unfortunately, he'd found out as soon as she'd been promoted to the next grade that beauty really was only skin deep.

"YOU LOOK LIKE SOMEONE just killed your best dog," Jon said, pushing the door to the fort open, climbing up, and flopping down beside him. "Bad day?"

"You could say that."

When he didn't say anything else, Jon just lay there staring at him. It was a trick he must have learned from Dan, who was probably the most patient person Sam had ever met. He could sit and look at you, not saying a word, waiting for you to spill your guts. And everyone always spilled them, just to make him stop. Jon was almost that good and no matter how much Sam wanted to win this battle of wills, he knew he wouldn't. Jon would just out wait him.

"Stop it," he muttered, clamping his lips together.

"Stop what?"

He could hear it in his voice, a hint of amusement because he knew exactly what he was doing—and that Sam was powerless to stop him. And he was right.

About thirty seconds later, the words came pouring out of his mouth. He hadn't even lasted a minute. By the time he'd finished his sad, miserable tale, he was scrubbing at his eyes like a little girl.

"I thought she was going to invite me for supper. She said her parents wanted to meet me. But- She didn't say anything about it. Just showed me the note from the teacher on the last day of summer school. She told me she didn't need any more help and then took off to tell her friends.

"That's not the worst part though. I went to her house this afternoon. I wanted to see if everything was all right. She—she just laughed. She called me a sucker and slammed the door in my face. She just used me to pass the math class. That's all she wanted from me. And then she dumped me...

Of course, it was hard to dump someone you hadn't actually been dating. No matter how real it had been for him, he'd been the only one who cared. All she'd wanted was a passing grade. And after she'd gotten it, had actually gotten it more than a week ago, she'd gone back to pretending like he didn't exist.

Yeah, he was a sucker all right. He just didn't fit in. Not with girls anyway. Well this was it for him. He was done with them. Forever. Broken hearts hurt way too much. And talk about the humiliation... Yeah. He didn't need that again either. Females just weren't worth it.

Jon finally turned his head, staring up at the ceiling now and Sam breathed a silent sigh of relief. Not just because he didn't feel like a target anymore but because it felt good to tell someone what a rotten person Deirdre was.

"That's rough."

Sam eased back until he was lying on the floor too, wishing it had been Dan who'd come today. Not that Jon wasn't one of his best friends because he was. But Dan would have kept talking, trying to make him feel better. It probably wouldn't have helped but it would have been nice to have someone care enough to try.

"I figure I'm safe from ever getting hurt like that." Jon's voice broke the quiet once more. "Except for you, Dan, and Cal, I'm never going to care about anyone enough so they can hurt me. You might consider giving that a try."

The way he was feeling this afternoon, Sam seriously considered that option. It might beat having your heart crushed like a pop can. It would mean spending his life alone though. He wasn't sure he was ready to commit to that just yet. But writing girls off forever wasn't off the table either.

"You want to play catch?" Jon asked after a while. "This is kind of boring."

"Sure." Might as well. He was going to be miserable no matter what he did so getting in a little extra practice couldn't hurt.

An hour later, his arm and shoulder ached. He wasn't sure why but the longer they played, the madder he'd gotten, and the madder he'd gotten, the harder he'd thrown the ball. And for some reason, it helped, especially when he pictured Jon's glove as Deirdre's heart. Just thinking about battering hers as badly as she'd battered his made him feel a little better.

"Boys, supper is ready!"

Jon closed the glove around the ball he'd just caught, tucked it under his arm, and started rubbing his palm. Sam hoped he hadn't hurt it too much, but if he had, why was Jon wearing such a self-satisfied look?

And then he realized that in his own way, Jon had done as much—or more—than Dan would have. He might not be comfortable talking about broken hearts but it seemed he knew a thing or two about working sad and angry feelings out of his system.

"I guess I'm invited for supper," he said, as they walked to the house, pretending like he hadn't just helped Sam in his first steps toward learning to deal with girls.

IT WAS ALSO THE SUMMER Cal hadn't been able to decide whether he hated his brother or not.

For some reason, Kelly Junior's seventeenth birthday had arrived with a newly acquired mean streak. Not all of the time but enough that Cal never knew from day to day what Kelly's mood was going to be—or if *he* was going to be the target of another insult or butt of a joke.

"IT'S ABOUT TIME, RUNT," Kelly said, reaching out to ruffle Cal's hair on his way out of the bathroom. "Did you leave me any hot water?"

"Stop calling me that," Cal muttered, ducking away from his hand, even though it meant bumping into the wall to get away from him.

"Why? It's true. Unless some miracle happens, you're always going to be short so you better get used to it. And if you are hoping for that miracle, you better not hold your breath. You take after Mom and Dad. I take after Grandpa Walker. You guys were destined to be little freaks. I, on the other hand, turned out normal." With a superior grin, he closed himself in the bathroom. After scowling at the door for a moment, Cal walked to his room, shoulders slumped, steps slow.

Flopping down on his bed, he laid back and let his feet dangle. Of course they didn't touch the floor. Not even his toes. What else did he expect though? A runt's feet never touched the floor like a regular guy's did. Like all of his friends' did. Like his bratty big brother's did.

Three years older, Kelly Junior was a star football player, popular, and everything Cal could never hope to be. Sometimes, he almost hated him. Even when Kelly was being nice, there was always a little cruelty to whatever he said and did. And sometimes it seemed his only mission in life was to make Cal's life hell on earth.

Other times, when anyone else picked on him, Kelly was his strongest champion. If anyone was going to be unkind to him, it wasn't going to be a stranger, or even someone they knew but who wasn't related. And when he needed help with things like catching or hitting a softball, it was his brother who stepped in to make sure he learned right.

Cal never knew what to think about him. Whether he should hate him for the incessant teasing, or just keep looking up to him like he was a hero.

Shaking his head, he jumped up and pulled a pair of jeans and a sweatshirt from his dresser. There was no time to think about the butthead down the hall. Maybe tomorrow his brother would be nice again, maybe he wouldn't.

So he wasn't going to care. He was just going to meet the guys for practice, then he, Dan, and Sam would head to their fort in the woods on the Jensen's property. They were going to talk about the birthday party they were having for Jon. He'd be turning fourteen in a couple of days and if they didn't do something, there would be no celebration.

Sam's parents were going to let them have a bonfire and sleepover. So far, everyone had been able to keep it a secret from Jon. Dan had already asked the Rambo's permission and extracted a promise to keep it a secret. It was going to be great! He and the guys had all been doing extra chores to earn money and had bought him a totally cool tool box—and a bunch of tools to put in it too.

If there was anything Jon liked to do, it was to fix or build things. Between him—and Sam, who had designed the fort—they had the most awesome place to hang out in the whole county. Probably in the whole state.

In minutes, he was tying his shoelaces and tearing off down the stairs. He didn't want to be late. Today was the day they would be meeting the new coach.

Mr. Nelson's boss had transferred him to Grand Rapids so less than a month into the season, whoever was in charge of the summer leagues had to find someone to fill in for him. Some of the guys were saying it was some big shot from a real ball team but he figured it was just the cop from Lansing he'd heard some of the parents talking about a few days ago. They'd said he lived over by Diamondale or Potterville, which still made him a resident of the county.

If it was a cop, he figured any fun they might have had was over.

HE'D BEEN WRONG THOUGH, Cal thought, shaking off memories from that summer and getting up from the table to stretch his legs.

Chris said he needed a quick bathroom break and everyone decided a snack break was in order too. Cal agreed, heading to the kitchen to pre-heat the oven

He pulled four packages of phyllo dough cups and a dish of spiced shredded beef and gravy from the fridge. It didn't take long to fill the cups and pop them in the oven. After setting the timer, he grabbed bowls of artichoke dip and crab salad and a tray of crackers to put out on the counter.

"Jon's going to be sorry he missed this," Dan said half an hour later, snatching a sesame cracker from the tray. Sam watched him scoop up a healthy mound of crab salad with it. Cal scowled, then grinned.

"Double dip and you'll live to regret it," he threatened, handing him a paper plate. "And save some for Jon. He'll be back."

Sam knew he'd make sure there was plenty of food for Jon when he got back though. Dan had long ago appointed himself a kind of papa bear to all of them. That was how Sam actually came to be a part of their group.

Before that day, he'd been a loner, just hanging out with his family. The kids he'd been friends with had stopped hanging out with him long before he'd been moved ahead three grades. He'd always figured it was because all the grownups started calling him a genius. Now he was stuck with kids a lot older than him. Kids he had nothing in common with. He wished he'd never taken the stupid tests.

After two months, he hadn't made a single friend. There was no recess either. Just one class after another, only broken up by lunch. He'd hated lunch period because every day he sat by himself, pretending to study, hoping the other kids weren't staring like they'd done the first week.

Some of them were worse than others though and he couldn't stop the memories from rolling through his head like a projector in his old science and health classes.

SAM CLOSED HIS EYES when he heard the footsteps echoing in the silent hall behind him. It was Bobby and his friends. He just knew it. They knew Miss Peters had kept him after class to talk about a new assignment and they'd waited for him. They always waited for him. Even though his coat was still in the locker and the late October day was chilly, he left it there,

closing the door as fast as he could. The clank of metal against metal sounded loud without dozens of other students laughing and talking to muffle it.

But maybe he could get away before they got to him. If he could just get around the corner, he could make a run for the principal's office. Except he hadn't gone two steps before he felt Bobby's hand on his shoulder, before his quiet, evil chuckle filled the hallway.

"Going somewhere, freak?" he asked, his fingers digging into Sam's shoulders.

"H-home. I'm going home," Sam stammered, wishing the words didn't sound shaky. Why, oh why had his parents ever thought jumping ahead three grades would be a good idea? Most of the kids ignored him. Why couldn't these guys?

"What? You were going to leave without telling us goodbye?" Bobby spun him around and slammed him against the lockers, leaning so close Sam could feel hot, stinky breath on his face.

"Goodbye?" he said hopefully.

"Not just yet, little boy. We need to have a talk."

There were murmurs of agreement from Bobby's small band of cohorts, followed by laughs and fists smacking palms. Sam wondered if today would be the day they stopped with the threats and finally beat him up.

"What- What do you want to talk about?" he whispered, his eyes wide with fear.

"You're making us look bad, genius. I'll bet you still wet the bed but you're getting better grades than we are. And we're tired of it. We're tired of Miss Peters telling us what a good student you are and we should all work harder to be like you."

"What do you want me to do?"

"Stop being so smart!"

"I—don't know how." If he did, he would, and then maybe they'd put him back in sixth grade. Oh how he wished he could go back there!

"Start failing tests or something. I don't care. Just stop getting all A's. Understand?" He thumped his finger hard against his head and Sam winced from the pain.

"I—"

"Hey, Sam," a voice at the end of the hall said. "What's taking you so long? We're all waiting, man. Come on. Shake a leg."

Sam turned to see one of the guys in his class—he thought his name might be Dan—standing there, hands on his hips and looking impatient. Bobby stepped back a few inches, not far enough but at least their noses weren't almost touching now.

"Hey, Mulholland. We're having a talk here. Why don't you take a hike?"

"Sorry," Dan said, sauntering closer, his smile disappearing. "It doesn't look like my friend wants to talk to you so maybe you should take a walk. A long one. Off a short pier. Or maybe I could go and get Jon. It looks like the two of you probably need to have a talk."

Sam noticed that Bobby's face paled a little and this time, he took a few steps back. He tried to remember who Jon was but couldn't put a face to the name. Bobby knew who he was though. Obviously. He seemed to be afraid of him too and that's all that mattered.

"Oh go ahead and rescue another misfit. We'll get him someday."

"Then we'll get you."

Bobby's hands curled into fists as he glared at Dan for a few seconds, then he turned and stomped away, the half dozen boys who practically worshiped him scurrying after him.

"Thanks," Sam murmured, looking at his feet in shame.

"No problem," Dan said, slinging an arm around his shoulders. "C'mon. Get your coat. They won't be bothering you again. I promise."

"They'll just come back tomorrow," he said, opening the locker again and putting his coat on.

"No they won't."

The arm went around his shoulders again and they headed toward the front doors and out of the school. Sam wanted to believe him but the next time Bobby caught him alone, he was going to get it. Bad.

At least it was another day over and he hadn't been slugged. There was that.

Sixth grade might have been boring but at least most of the other kids hadn't hated him. Not this much anyway. And he'd been allowed to hang out with some of the other geeky kids sometimes. They weren't friends, and they didn't talk much but at least when they sat together in the lunch room, it looked like it to everyone else.

"Don't let 'em get to you," Dan was saying, bringing him back to the present as he reached out to push the door open. "They're just stupid. They know you're going to grow up, get rich, and make them look bad because all they're going to be doing is making hamburgers or shoveling horse poop. That's why they don't like you. They're jealous because you'll have it made and they won't."

He sure hoped Dan was right. But there were a lot of years between now and then and Bobby—and other boys like him—were going to make his life miserable. Why couldn't he have just been born normal, like everyone else?

They approached two other guys. One of them was a little shorter than he was and Sam didn't have a clue who he was. The other guy was taller and looked stronger than all the rest of them put together. He assumed that was Jon, the guy Bobby was so afraid of. Looking at him, he could understand why.

"Hey, guys. You know who Sam is, right? He's going to be hanging out with us from now on." Dan looked at the tallest one. "Jon? Bobby Danvers doesn't like him."

"Bobby and his minions been giving you trouble?" Jon asked. Sam nodded and watched him grin. "Well, they won't be giving you anymore after today. I guarantee it."

Cal, the shortest one of the group, told him that Bobby and his friends had set their sights on him a few years ago. Dan had rescued him too. They all thought Bobby would back off, but he hadn't. He and Jon wound up in a fight. Jon won and Bobby had been scared of him ever since.

LOOKING AT HIS FRIENDS now, sitting around the table chowing down on their snacks and talking and laughing, Sam was grateful. He'd always been grateful for them. Everyone always said they didn't know where Jon would be today without all of them but he didn't know where he'd be today if Dan hadn't intervened that afternoon. Certainly not here with these men he was closer to than his own brother.

IT MUST BE THE NIGHT for reminiscing, Dan thought as he piled snacks on his plate, especially the treat his lovely wife had surprised him with. Cal, ever the chef, frowned in disgust but Dan was always going to love bacon. And when Jess wrapped thick slices around tiny little smoked breakfast sausages and baked them to greasy perfection, he was in heaven. It was probably a good thing she only made them for him a couple of times a year.

Moving down the line, he grabbed a few cherry tomatoes and green pepper slices, partly to prove he liked healthy foods too but mostly to get Cal to stop frowning.

Maybe he wasn't frowning at his plate though because his gaze never moved from where Dan had been standing. Maybe, like him, he was thinking about Jon, whose evening had been interrupted by parents who had never wanted a child. Or if they had, the novelty had worn off and they'd changed their minds.

By the time school brought them together, Jon had already learned that if he didn't take care of himself, no one else would.

Fortunately, some things had changed. Not enough though. While he learned he wasn't quite as alone as he'd thought, he was still stuck in a bad situation with no real way out. Not then anyway.

They'd all felt so helpless back then. Him, the other guys, even their parents. They knew what was going on but Jon blamed it on him being clumsy. Even when someone, Mrs. Jensen, they thought, called Protective Services, Jon said they were nuts. His parents were like the Cleavers. Perfect in every way.

As they got older, Dan came to realize that Jon was scared. If he owned up to what was going on at his house, he might be put in foster care. And he might not be put somewhere in Charlotte. Charlotte was where his friends were and they were all he had.

His thoughts drifted back to the summer when all but Sam turned fourteen.

"HI, MRS. RAMBO," DAN said, forcing himself to smile at the woman peering out from a narrow crack between the door and the frame.

She looked like she hadn't brushed her hair since—well, he didn't know when. She probably hadn't slept much over the weekend either since that was prime party time. The stink rolling off her clothes was enough to make him gag, but he kept the smile pasted on his face.

"What do you want, Dan?" she asked. It was clear it took every ounce of control she possessed to keep her tone polite. Or as polite as she could ever manage.

"My dad said he'd give me 'n Jon each twenty dollars if we'd do some yard work at one of his houses. If Jon can come along with us."

"Twenty dollars?" Her attitude perked up at that.

"Yes, ma'am. We might be late so Dad said he could just spend the night at our house. If that's all right with you."

"I'm sure Jon would love to help you out. I'll just go get him for you."

She would take the twenty when Jon went home the next day. She always did. That's why Dan and his father worked out a deal. Technically, what he'd just told Mrs. Rambo was the truth. His dad would give him the money. But he was actually paying Jon forty so he could keep the second twenty.

Jon hated having to take their charity but Nate Mulholland said the boys did the work of two men and eighty bucks was a deal for him. Besides, it was the only way they could make sure Jon had more than just the hit and miss meals his parents provided—after spending the bulk of their income on beer.

Except Dan was sure they were getting buzzed on more than that. They didn't make as much money as his dad but they both worked the night shift at one of the local factories and they paid fairly well. Even with the two of them getting drunk as skunks every day, they couldn't be spending that much on beer so he figured they were probably using drugs too.

When Jon didn't come to the door right away, Dan started pacing on the wooden front porch that ran the full length of the house. For as long as they'd been friends, and that had been from the first day of kindergarten, it had needed paint. The whole house needed paint but it hadn't seen a fresh coat even once in the nine years since then.

"Hey," Jon said from behind him. Dan whirled around and had to clench his teeth together. Another bruise was forming on his cheek, and he'd missed a spot of blood beside his nose. "Sorry it took me so long. I was in such a hurry I slipped on the rug in my room. Got a darned bloody nose. That took a while to stop. Sorry."

"It's okay," Dan muttered, scowling at the door and wishing Jon would just tell the truth.

No one could do anything to help if he kept making up stories like this one. They both knew he didn't have a rug in his room, just as they both knew that when he said it happened—again—that meant he wasn't talking about what really happened this time either.

"You gotta be more careful," was all he could think to say. Jon just shrugged, smacked his arm lightly, and changed the subject.

"So where's this job?"

"In Lansing. Dad'll be home soon. He said we'd pick up burgers on the way."

"Cool. Let's get going then."

Jon slung a faded, frayed backpack, stuffed with a change of clothes, over his shoulder and they trotted down the steps and headed for the Mulholland house on Sheldon Row. Not quite a mile from the Rambo house on McClure, it wasn't long before they were sitting on the deck off the kitchen at Dan's. His mom brought them each a glass of lemonade and a big bowl of nacho chips to snack on while they waited.

His parents made it their mission to stuff as many calories as they could into Jon every time an opportunity presented itself. Sam and Cal's parents did the same and Dan was grateful to them all for trying to help his friend.

"So I've been reading some interesting information about jobs in the south," Jon said after a few minutes of silence. Silence spent pretending Dan was as hungry as Jon as they scarfed the chips down. "Even some places out west."

"What about it?" He was starting to feel a little sick and was sorry he'd eaten the greasy chips. He knew what was coming, and that he wasn't going to like it. In fact, he was probably going to hate it.

"They don't ask questions in some places. I mean, anyone can find work—even kids like me. They don't care who you are or where you're from. You just sign your name—and it doesn't have to be your real name either because they don't check you out. Then you start picking fruits and vegetables and they pay you in cash. Not what the jobs are worth, for sure, but better than nothing. It'd be hard work but I could do it."

"You mean—" He'd known what Jon was going to say but he still felt like someone slugged him in the gut. It was as bad—and worse—than he'd expected. "You're thinking about leaving? By yourself?"

"Not until next year. I'll be fifteen then. That would give me time to save money from working for your dad, mowing lawns, and shoveling snow. I wouldn't want to leave without enough to get me by until I could find a place to stay. And find a job."

"No." Dan was shaking his head. "No. You don't want to do that. We'll figure something else out."

What that something else might be, he didn't have a clue. All he could think of was that his friend's life was so bad he wanted to run away. And not just run away but run far away. As in they might not ever see him again.

There isn't another way. And it's not like it would be forever. I figure by the time I'm eighteen, I'd have saved enough for college and could come back then. Just like we planned."

"I've read about those jobs too," Dan murmured, staring Jon straight in the eye. "They don't even pay minimum wage, and the people have to work from the time the sun comes up until it goes down. They barely make enough to survive. How would you be able to save money for college? And when would you have time to go to school so you could get your diploma? Because MSU isn't going to take you without one."

"Night school."

"Don't you have to be a grownup to go to night school?"

"I don't know. If I can get down there, I'll figure something out."

"Hey, guys, ready to go?" Nate Mulholland asked, sticking his head out the sliding glass door and putting an end to their conversation.

"Sure, Dad," Dan said, pushing away from the table and getting to his feet.

"Don't tell anyone," Jon muttered. "Not even Cal and Sam."

"I won't."

And he would do his best to keep his mouth shut. At least that's what he kept telling himself. Even after their short break when they were half finished with the mowing. Jon must not have been thinking too clearly in the heat of the day because he raised the hem of his tee shirt to wipe the sweat from his face. Dan saw the purple and yellow bruises covering his ribs just before their eyes met. Jon just shrugged, dropped the shirt, and took a long swallow of water.

AFTER FILLING THEIR plates and settling back down at the table, they continued to reminisce about the old days.

"Do you remember when I first took over the team?" Ed asked, chuckling when he looked at Cal, whose face turned a little red at the memory.

"I do." Sam snickered when he looked at his friend. "Cal wasn't the only one who thought our fun on the field was over when a *cop* took over the team though."

"I think you're being a little generous calling it a team," Ed said. "You guys were the worst in the league that summer. Not that it was your fault. I don't know who recruited the first guy but he had no business even *saying* the word softball much less trying to coach a bunch of kids."

Nods of agreement went round the table and they were all lost in thought again.

SAM ARRIVED AT THE ball field before anyone else, mostly because he'd busted his butt to get his chores finished early. He didn't want to be late today. Not that he ever was but like everyone else, he was anxious to see the new coach.

None of the guys knew what to think about a cop taking over. Some were bummed, some were nervous, others —the troublemakers — were a little scared. But he was more curious than anything. The dads who coached worked at different kinds of jobs but this was the first time they would have someone from a police department.

His mom heard he wasn't married so that was kind of weird. Why would a single guy take on the coaching of a bunch of kids he didn't even know? Had he gotten in trouble at work and this was his punishment? Maybe he'd lost a bet or drawn a short straw. If any of those kinds of scenarios came into play, it could be a long summer. Guys who didn't really want to coach, like Mr. Nelson, didn't put much effort into it.

Cal was the next one from the team to arrive. He sat down beside him on the bench and started swinging his feet. Cal, the shortest of all the players on the Charlotte Stingers, was the only one who could do that but no one pointed it out to him. Most didn't have the heart. The rest kept quiet because they knew they'd have him, Dan, and Jon to deal with. Besides, it wasn't like he was a troll or anything, he was just—shorter than the rest of them.

"He's not here yet?" Cal asked, though it was obvious they were the only ones anywhere near the field.

"Na. We're about half an hour early. Shouldn't be long though."

"Think he'll be any good?"

"I don't know. He can't be any worse than Mr. Nelson." And that was the truth. They played twenty-two games every summer. Last year, they'd only won two. So far this season, they'd played three and lost them all.

"Think he'll ruin everything? You know, being a cop and all."

"I don't know. A lot of cops are pretty cool," drawled a deep voice from behind them. Sam looked at Cal and swallowed hard. The new coach had finally arrived. Talk about bad luck. "I'm Ed Winslow," the man in question said, walking around to stand in front of them. He stuck out a hand and shook both of theirs.

"Sorry about—what I said," Cal stammered, and Sam saw that his face was about as red as the fire trucks in the bay at the station downtown.

"Don't worry about it. When I was your age, I didn't trust cops much either. Truth be told, I still don't trust some of them." He slung a leg over the bench, straddling the wooden plank when he sat down. "What position do you two play?"

"Second base," Sam told him, then watched Cal turn a darker shade of red when he muttered, "shortstop." From the way Officer Winslow's lips thinned out, he wondered if the new coach knew Mr. Nelson put him there as kind of a joke.

"Well, I hope you're not too attached to those positions. Given your win/loss record, we'll be trying everyone out in all positions so we know where your strengths are."

Cal looked relieved and he didn't blame him but Sam hoped he didn't get moved. He actually played pretty well on second. He was comfortable there.

He also hoped that the coach wouldn't look too close at their personal information. It had taken a lot of talking on his father's part to get him on this particular team. Being two and a half years younger, he should have been on the little kids' team, but since he'd been moved ahead to the same grade the other guys were in and they were such great friends, he'd been allowed to play here. The other coach's hadn't liked it but they hadn't cared enough to put up a fuss about it either.

"Do you think any of you boys will object to practicing three or four times a week?" Winslow was asking, bringing Sam out of his thoughts. "I don't think we've got enough time to get you in the playoffs this year but I think we can move you up in the ranks—if you're willing to work for it."

Sam was impressed. This man already showed more enthusiasm for the game, and the team, than Mr. Nelson had in two years. When they both said they didn't have a problem with it, he suggested they move to the field.

"We'll do some batting practice. You can show me what you've got."

As more boys showed up, including Dan and Jon about twenty minutes later, they were added to the field, each one taking a turn at home plate, as well as different positions on the field with each new batter. After a couple of hours, Officer Winslow, who had begun taking notes as soon as he was able to stop pitching, called them all over to the dugout to tell them what their new, temporary positions were, and to let them know they'd start practicing in earnest every Saturday, and two weekday evenings.

Sam was thrilled when Cal got put in right field. He wasn't the greatest player on the team but he did all right. A lot better catching pop ups there than fast grounders where he had been, that was for sure. All in all, it looked like they might finish the season closer to the middle than the bottom. It would be really nice for a change.

OVER THE YEARS, ED had been tempted to look for Karl Nelson, just to see what kind man he was when dealing with adults. But those thoughts had been short lived because he didn't really care. If Nelson had any kind of integrity, Ed would never have met these guys and he'd always be grateful for the opportunity that had been offered to him. They deserved the best now, just as they'd deserved it then.

ED TOOK THE LAST QUARTER of the Jersey Giant sub sandwich he'd picked up a few days ago from the fridge, slapped it on a paper plate, grabbed a bottle of cola and a banana, and sat down at the table in the tiny dining room to go over his notes about the team.

It was hard for him to believe that any man who had even the most infinitesimal amount of knowledge about the game could have been such an idiot. But that title seemed to fit Mr. Nelson to a tee.

After just one afternoon with the team, he'd had a pretty good idea of each boy's strengths. By the third practice, he'd moved them around again, putting them in the positions they were best suited for. Now, Ed knew they had a chance to start winning at least a few games.

Or at least they had a reason to hope anyway and when they left the field to head home today, their attitudes had changed from resignation to cautious optimism.

Except for four of them. He took a bite of the sandwich, chewing it slowly as he stared out the sliding glass doors across the room. Those particular boys seemed to approach everything with enthusiasm—whether their odds of winning were zero or seventy percent.

Dan Mulholland seemed to be the glue that held them together. He was a mother hen kind of guy who probably spent too much time worrying over his buddies than was normal for a kid his age.

Jon Rambo, a tough one who Ed suspected had a less than loving home, was the self-appointed bodyguard. He had no doubt that if anyone started messing with one of his friends, they'd be dealing with him.

Cal O'Hara seemed to be the most insecure one of the bunch and one day, after his older brother had showed up to harass him, it was easy to see why. Shorter than most of his peers, but not abnormally so, Cal took a lot of ribbing. Short stuff, midget, Smurf. And that was just from his brother. Poor kid.

And then there was Sam Jensen. Shy, unsure, a little scared he'd be kicked off the team. More than two years younger than the other three, it was clear they were all especially protective of him. Ed was glad. He'd seen firsthand that 'normal' boys could make life hell on earth for nerdy geniuses, particularly those who had been promoted to higher grades with older kids.

Some might call them a peculiar group but it did his heart good to see the camaraderie and loyalty in four youngsters. Usually, he only saw that kind of closeness in groups of kids that could best be described as troublemakers. That was definitely not the case with these boys.

NATE MULHOLLAND AND Kelly O'Hara had been playing in a mid-afternoon bowling tournament so they were about an hour late to the game. Dan let them in, then led the way to the dining area after hanging their coats in the closet.

"Snacks are in the kitchen, guys," Cal told them, nodding toward the counter. "We're taking a little break."

"Yeah," Ed said. "Reminiscing about the summer I took over the boys' softball team.

"That was quite the summer," Nate said, the smile he'd been wearing dimming a bit as he grabbed a plate from the stack near the stove.

Dan noticed everyone glanced discreetly at Kelly but his expression didn't give away anything. Of course, it had been a couple of decades so the pain wouldn't be as bad as it had then. And it had been bad. He should know. He'd witnessed it firsthand...

"OH MAN, I'M STARVING," Dan said, putting the kickstand down with his heel. "Are you sure your mom won't mind if we raid the fridge?"

"Na. The only reason she got mad before is because she was planning to use that leftover roast to make burritos. She'll be cool with it today though." He laughed then said, "As long as we don't eat anything that looks like she's going to use it for supper."

Dan remembered the last time and hoped he was right. While Mrs. O'Hara hadn't yelled or thrown anything, she had that look all mothers get when they'd like to throttle you. She really hadn't been happy to find they'd used the beef to make sandwiches either. Not just for them, but for Jon and Sam too. And they'd eaten every bite.

But he was right. The O'Hara's were pretty cool and never seemed to mind when he or any of the guys showed up. And Dan sure hoped she had some food they could eat because Mr. Winslow had busted their butts at practice today. It was paying off though. After only a few weeks, they'd won a couple of games and he was confident they'd win the one tomorrow night.

"C'mon. I'm starving." Cal grabbed his sleeve and pulled him toward the house.

The first thing they heard when they walked in the door was the sound of his mother crying. Hard. His dad was saying stuff, trying to comfort her, Dan thought. He couldn't hear any words but that's what it sounded like.

He looked at Cal and Cal looked at him and he supposed they both looked a little scared. More uncomfortable though. Sometimes his folks argued and his mother would cry and it was just weird to be there when it happened.

"How will we tell Cal?" he heard her ask, then start to cry harder, and then Dan wasn't uncomfortable anymore. He was just scared for his friend. Were his parents getting a divorce? But if they were, would Mr. O'Hara be trying to be nice to her? He didn't think so.

Cal looked like he wanted to be anywhere except here but he started walking toward the kitchen, his steps slow like he didn't want to move at all. Kind of like his feet seemed to be moving by themselves. Dan's did too because he couldn't seem to stop his from following his friend.

When they got to the doorway, he could see Cal's folks hugging each other, that his dad was crying too, and he knew whatever the news was, it was going to be really bad. Like the worst news anyone could ever get.

And he was right.

When Mr. O'Hara spotted them, he held out his hand like he wanted Cal to come over but Cal shook his head and demanded to know what was wrong. For a minute, Dan didn't think Mr. O'Hara was going to answer, then he took a deep breath and said,

"There—there was an accident, son. Your brother- Kelly-" He shoved his fist against his mouth and Mrs. O'Hara's knees gave out. She'd have fallen to the floor if her husband hadn't been holding her so tight.

"Where's Kelly?" Cal whispered, taking a couple of steps backward, right into Dan, who put his hands on his shoulders to stop him. "Where's my brother?"

"Cal—" Mr. O'Hara said, then stopped for a few more seconds before he said, his voice so quiet Dan could hardly hear him, "I'm sorry. I'm so sorry. Kelly died."

For a moment, Dan wondered if Cal was going to say anything. He just stood there like a statue, staring at his parents. Then he started shaking his head.

"No!" he shouted, and his volume increased with every word after that. "No! You're lying! He's not dead! Why would you say something like that?" And then he turned, shoving Dan out of the way and running through the house shouting Kelly's name over and over.

Mr. O'Hara sat his wife in a kitchen chair and told Dan to stay with her as he went in search of Cal. Not knowing what else to do, Dan nodded, though he'd rather be anywhere but in a room alone with a mother whose son had just died. It didn't matter though, because she laid her head on the table and kept crying. He didn't know what to do. Whether he should stay where he was or maybe walk over to her and pat her shoulder or—something. In the end, he just stood there.

"He's not dead!" Cal screamed from the front of the house. A door slammed and Mr. O'Hara hurried back to the kitchen. It was clear he didn't want to leave his wife but he was worried about his son—now his only living son—too. "He's taken off on his bike. I need to get the car."

Dan didn't stand around to hear more, just said he needed to go, and then he left, jumping on his bike and taking off after his friend.

Cal was already a couple of blocks ahead of him and Dan had to pedal harder than he'd ever done before to catch up. When he finally did, Cal stopped and same as in the kitchen, he didn't know what to do. Especially not when Cal picked his bike up and threw it as hard as he could at a tree, then sat down in the grass beside it.

He was sobbing, saying over and over that his brother wasn't dead but Dan knew he was just lying to himself. He knew his dad had told him the truth. Cal just didn't want to believe it. But if someone told him Bruce had died, he supposed he wouldn't want to believe it either.

Knowing he couldn't leave before Mr. O'Hara got there, he just sat down beside Cal and started rubbing his back. He didn't know what to say so he didn't say anything at all.

ED NOTED THAT DAN LOOKED surprised when Jon rejoined them at the table. He'd been lost in thought and was pretty sure he knew the reason why. Fortunately, no one else seemed to have noticed. But then it wasn't unusual for Dan to get lost in thought so even if they had, they wouldn't have thought much of it.

It was hard though to look back at that year and not remember the bad and the sad with the good. It had been rough for Sam to experience his first broken heart, and it had been miserable for Dan to see so many hurtful things happening to his friends and not be able to do anything about it.

Ed always figured that's why Dan had broken his promise. So much had been beyond his control, so much he couldn't fix. And when it seemed as though he might lose one of his friends, he couldn't stand it anymore.

ED SLOWED HIS CAR TO a crawl. It looked like Dan Mulholland up ahead but since he'd never seen the boy without at least one of his buddies, he figured it must be another kid. One who looked exactly like him, only this one was walking, shoulders slumped like he was either exhausted or it was the end of the world. And Dan never walked that way. Nope. His shoulders were always squared back, his step a mixture of confidence and enthusiasm. Exactly the opposite of this boy, so it couldn't be Dan.

Except it was.

He pulled the car to the curb, flipping the button on his door to roll the window down.

"Hey," he called out. Dan looked up and Ed could have sworn he'd never seen such a despondent expression on any kid's face. "Why don't you hop in? We can go for a ride."

Dan stood there, as though trying to decide what he should do, then with a shrug, he crossed the grassy strip between the sidewalk and road, opened the door, and sunk down in the seat. It looked to Ed as though he'd curled in on himself and, uncharacteristically, he didn't say a word.

"Going anywhere in particular?" he asked, checking for traffic in his side mirror, then pulling back out into the lane.

"No."

"Then we'll just ride around until you're ready to go home, okay?"

"Yeah. Thanks."

All the boys knew if they needed to talk, he'd listen—and Dan needed to talk, so he just drove slowly around town, down one side road after another, waiting patiently, hoping he'd be able to help with whatever it was that was bothering him. After about twenty minutes, Dan whispered,

"Jon's going to run away."

Ed's breath hitched. There was no doubt that young man had a rough life, though he'd never admit it to anyone. And until he did, there really wasn't anything anyone could do to help. Except it seemed Jon was going to take matters into his own hands rather than do any asking.

"When?"

"When school lets out for the summer."

He breathed a sigh of relief. Eight months away. There was time.

"So he's just planning it right now?"

"No. He already has a plan. He's just doing jobs for my dad and other people and saving his money right now."

"Where's he planning to go?"

"Down south." Something in his tone caused Ed to glance over at him and he watched Dan wipe at his eyes. "He says—he's going to get a job working in fields. He says he's heard they don't care how young you are and they don't ask questions. They just pay in cash every day."

"I've heard that too." Things must be worse than he'd thought if Jon was planning to travel so far to get away from his parents. It wasn't going

to happen though. He reached across the seat and squeezed Dan's shoulder. "We'll figure something out, okay? Don't worry. He's not going anywhere."

"You don't know Jon. He will."

"Trust me, okay? I'll come up with a better plan."

And he would because there was no way he was going to allow that kid to ruin his life. It just wasn't going to happen. Not on his watch.

It had taken him a few hours to figure out what he needed to do and, having settled on a plan that wouldn't implicate Dan, he saw no reason to delay putting it into action.

First thing this morning, Ed called in to take a personal day, then waited until he knew for sure the boys were in class before calling Dan, Sam, and Cal's parents. He needed to make sure they were on board with it and was pleased when they all but cheered when he laid it all out for them.

And now, here he was, standing on the porch of a house that had been neglected for too long. He'd bet, from the way the paint was peeling on the faded wood siding, that it hadn't seen a fresh coat in more than a decade.

"Mr. Rambo?" he asked when an unshaven man who smelled as though he hadn't bathed in a while opened the front door. He looked at Ed, his brows raised in suspicion.

"Who wants to know?"

"I'm Ed Winslow. Jon's softball coach. I wondered if we could have a talk about your son."

"I thought softball season was over."

"We still practice, and will continue to do so until winter sets in. Could I come in please?"

"We signed the permission slip, what's there to talk about?"

"I'm afraid there's a problem. I won't take up much of your time."

With a roll of his eyes, Carl Rambo finally relented and opened the door. The stench about knocked Ed over as he stepped across the threshold. From what he could see, the living room wasn't too filthy but he'd bet the same couldn't be said of the kitchen. Still, that wasn't why he was here.

"*Does my wife need to be here too?*" *the man asked, rubbing a hand over the stained tee shirt that hung loosely over his small pot belly.*

"*It would help, yes.*"

"*Have a seat then,*" *Carl said, nodding toward the living room. It was filled with an assortment of sofas and chairs in various states of decay and it broke Ed's heart to think that this was the place Jon had to call home.*

Ed opted to stand while his host went to the foot of the stairs and bellowed for Benita to come down. A woman's voice, ugly and ornery, answered back that she was trying to sleep. He yelled that Jon's coach was here and she needed to come down. Now. After a short silence, he heard some thumping and complaining, but in short order, both of them joined him in the living room.

They made a sorry pair, their hair greasy and uncombed, clothes wrinkled and dirty. He'd seen enough in his career to know it happened with far too much regularity but this was the first time he'd seen it when it affected someone he cared about.

"*Have a seat.*" *He waited until they complied, then stood before them and got down to business.* "*I'm not going to beat around the bush, and I'm not going to sugar coat what I'm going to say.*"

"*Huh?*" *Benita asked.*

"*Just shut up and listen.*"

"*You don't talk to my wife that way!*" *Carl started to say. When Ed moved his jacket to reveal the revolver strapped to his side, he sat back down, glaring at him.*

"*Here's the deal. I know you beat your son. I know you neglect him, and I know you don't feed him because you spend most of your money on beer. And probably drugs.*"

"*You don't know anything,*" *Benita snarled, cowering behind her husband's arm.*

"*Oh but I do. And I'm giving you one chance—one chance—to agree to a deal. I don't care if you drink or drug yourselves to death but if either one of you ever lays so much as a finger on that boy again, I'll see to it you're both* locked up. For a long time. Or worse." He made sure they could both see his revolver again.

"Are you threatening us?" This was from Carl.

"As a matter of fact, I am. But you're not going to do anything about it, are you? Because if you do, I'll have CPS here so fast it'll make your head spin. And I think we both know what their investigation will turn up, don't we?" He let that bit of information sink in before delivering the final blow. "What's more, if Jon wants to stay with me, or any of his friends, you're not going to give him a hard time. I don't care if he doesn't come home for a month—or six months, you're not going to do a thing to stop him. Are we clear?"

"My back is all screwed up. I can barely do my job. I need him to-"

"You know what? I. Don't. Care." Ed said, his voice low and menacing. He took a couple of steps closer to them, pleased when they cringed against the back of the sofa. "Like I said, this is the only chance you're getting. Are you going to agree to my terms, or—" He nodded at a dirty telephone on the table beside one of the sofas. "Do I call CPS now?"

"Whatever," Carl finally spat out. "We'll save money if we don't have to feed him, won't we?"

Ed had never wanted to hit someone as bad as he did in that moment but managed to restrain himself. He also bit his lip so he didn't point out that they rarely fed him anyway. There was no point. They'd agreed. That's all he'd wanted and that's what he got. Jon wouldn't have to run away now because he and everyone else would make sure he was safe, loved, and cared for.

"All right. Just make sure I don't have to come back. Because trust me, if you don't keep your word, I'll be your worst nightmare."

JON COULD TELL BY THE way Ed was looking at him that he was thinking about that summer. He wore the same expression every time he jumped when they called. It was always about money and none of them understood why he gave it to them.

Heck, he didn't really understand it himself. But it was what it was and he wasn't going to stop now. The paltry amount it cost him, a windfall for them, barely made a dent in his savings. And it usually kept them from bothering him for five or six months.

Sometimes, he wondered if Ed would tell him he'd given them enough, but he never said a word. Just watched him quietly, a lot like Dan sometimes did. He supposed if anyone had the right to say anything though, it would be this man. He'd always been a kind of surrogate father to him. Now he was his father-in-law.

Kind of fitting given what happened when he was a kid.

"... I'LL BE YOUR WORST nightmare."

Jon crept back to his room, tears streaming down his cheeks. His folks didn't know he was here. His ribs hurt too much from the beating he'd gotten last night. He'd scorched the tomato soup his mother ordered him to 'cook' and his father had gone berserk over it. So he'd skipped school today, curling up on a quilt in his dark closet, not making a sound so they wouldn't find him in case they looked in his room for some reason.

When he heard his father call out that his coach was here though, he'd crept to the top of the stairs to find out why. What he'd heard made him both sick with shame and weak with relief. He didn't know how the coach had known what was going on but things were going to be okay now. They really were.

He snuck back into the closet, sank down onto the quilt, held his pillow against his face, and began to sob quietly. He'd never have to come back, not if he didn't want to. They couldn't hurt him anymore. He wouldn't have to lie about where he got this bruise or that one, or why he was limping. Coach Winslow had made sure of that.

CHAOS ERUPTED AT THAT point as the front door burst open and a seemingly never ending stream of kids ran in, followed more slowly by their mothers.

Ed couldn't help but grin as he watched. Seven years ago, it had just been the six of them sitting around playing poker for peanuts. Now there were thirty-one of them, soon to be thirty-two when Chris and Harry's new baby arrived around Valentine's Day.

Of course, that number included new 'family' members, Nate and Monica Mulholland, Kelly O'Hara, Mitch and Clancy Montague and their little girl Lucy, and Ty and Emma Lanning and their little boy, Michael. While most everyone was here tonight, with the holidays so close, a few were missing as they visited with relatives or spent a few days at a big Florida amusement park—but they'd all be back in time for the annual Christmas Eve party next week.

Though they all had roomy houses, Dan sometimes mentioned that they should rent a hall because things were getting a bit crowded. Then he'd grin and shake his head because he wasn't fooling anyone. He loved having everyone he cared about within touching distance, even if that distance sometimes felt like a sardine can.

Five year old Tara was sitting in his lap now, showing him an angel she'd made from a paper plate, sequins, and cotton balls. Bailey, almost three now, was showing off a picture of herself in a frame made of glitter covered wooden craft sticks. Scotty, Brandon, and Benjamin followed their heroes, Zack and Billy, straight down to video game central in the basement.

"Where's Kate?" he asked, glancing around the room when he didn't see the seven year old ball of energy.

"She fell asleep in the car," Jess told him, smiling at him from where she stood behind Dan. "She's curled up on the couch, dreaming of sugar plums and fashion dolls." Everyone laughed. "So what did you guys do all night? Just play poker and eat the winnings?" she asked, glancing at the piles of candy.

"Actually," Dan said, "we took a little trip down memory lane too."

"Oh?"

"Yeah."

"Are you going to elaborate?" Holly wanted to know, carrying a stool from the kitchen bar to sit beside her husband.

"Just thinking back to the summer we all met Ed," Sam told her, reaching out for her hand.

"Everyone but Chris," Harry reminded them, brushing a hand softly through his hair.

"Yeah, we never did get to you," Jon said, turning his gaze to his partner.

"There's not much to tell," Chris mumbled, not meeting his eyes. He reached for the cards in the middle of the table and put them in a neat pile.

1997

Monroe, Michigan

"Time to eat, kiddo," Chris said, forcing a cheerfulness he didn't feel into his voice.

He sat the small tray on the dresser, then gently propped eight-year old Terri up so she was sitting, resting against a couple of pillows behind her back.

"I'm not hungry."

The softly spoken words were a familiar refrain, something he and his parents had heard several times a day since her chemo treatments started again.

"I don't blame you. Mom's chicken soup kind of sucks but she said if I could get you to eat half of what's in the bowl, four crackers, and most of the pudding, I could go rent a movie for us." He named one of their favorites—her favorite actually because he was too old for kiddie stuff—but if it meant getting some food down her, he'd watch it a hundred times.

Her lips turned down in a frown, her blue eyes moved from him to the tray he laid across her lap. She was torn, weighing throwing her lunch up—or at the very least, feeling queasy for the next couple of hours—against watching a beloved cartoon.

"You remember how we eat an elephant, right?" he teased, grinning when she giggled. He reached out and brushed dark hair away from her pale, too thin face.

"One bite at a time?"

"That's right. This-" he said, pointing at the tray, "is the elephant. This-" He held up a spoonful of soup, "is the first bite. Are we ready?"

He smile dimmed a little but after a moment, she nodded, and he spent the next half hour distracting her with all of the amusing stories he could remember about his friends, their neighbors, and people he'd seen around town. She gagged with almost every bite but until he heard 'the noise,' a low sound somewhere between her stomach and the back of her throat, the one that said one more bite was going to be one too many, he kept trying to get her to eat a little more.

He'd done it the first time the cancer invaded her tiny body at all of three years old. In fact, no one else had been able to get more food down her than him. It had been the same this time, after she'd lost half of the lower part of her leg.

Whatever it took though, he'd do. He wasn't going to lose his sister. That's just wasn't going to happen. Not if he had anything to do with it.

If he could get her to eat, get her to stay positive and focused on a happy future, even though she was scared right now, he'd give up everything else—for as long as it took. He'd watch every cartoon ever made. He'd sing every song she loved. He'd read stories to her until he was hoarse. Nothing else mattered as long as she was okay in the end.

BECAUSE SHE'D HAD AN altercation with a patient who annoyed her, Mary's day pass for Christmas had been revoked. So, since she couldn't come to the party, they brought the party, including supper, a small tree, and gifts to her. Ed and Jon paid monthly fees that bordered on robbery to make sure she had a private room and as long as they didn't bring sharp objects in, the staff allowed them to bring in pretty much whatever they wanted. In fact, they encouraged familial interaction for all of their patients which was one of the reasons they'd decided on this particular long-term care facility.

As violent incidents continued to decrease, her doctors were cautiously optimistic. Though she'd been here nearly five years, eventually, they promised, she'd be ready to move to an off-site assisted living home. It was a day Ed longed for. If she could just stop letting other patients like Toby, the guy who'd tried to strangle him a few years ago, get to her.

Still, she'd reached a place he'd never dreamed he'd see. Every time Ed watched Mary cradling her infant nephew, tears burned his eyes and a lump the size of Alaska lodged in his throat. From a crazed, drug addicted girl who wanted nothing more than to kill him to a doting aunt...

Yeah. Anyone who didn't believe in miracles needed witness her sitting in the rocker he'd bought her last summer, holding Nicky like he was a fragile piece of glass as she hummed Silent Night so softly he could barely hear her.

He watched his wife and youngest daughter as they watched her and noted their eyes were pretty bright. Even Jon seemed affected by the innocent beauty of a woman and a baby on this special Christmas Day. Except his way of being touched was to clench his teeth and stare out window covered with thick black chain link screen.

Eventually, Mary started getting restless. She was usually okay with company for two, sometimes three hours but four... Well that was a little more than she wanted to deal with. Reluctantly, she handed Nicky back to her sister while he, Jenna, and Jon started packing everything up.

It was always hard to leave her, especially on holidays, but Ed knew it was for the best. At least for the time being. It helped that she was close enough to visit a few times a week and as he stood last in line to tell her goodbye, he reminded himself he'd see her again on Wednesday.

Mary didn't always let him hug her but today, she actually wrapped her arms around his shoulders before he could even make an attempt to touch her. Another lump formed in his throat and he had to blink hard before she caught him and started teasing him about being a wimp.

"Thanks for coming," she said cheerfully, pressing her lips against his cheek.

"Merry Christmas, sweetheart. I love you so much." After a silence that stretched for what felt like forever, she said the words he hadn't heard in more than twenty years.

"I love you too, Daddy," Mary whispered. "Merry Christmas."

Get yummy recipes and fun notes from your favorite Coach's Boys stars in Cooking With the Coach's Boys by clicking here: http://kristykjames.net/books/ cooking-with-the-coachs-boys-hometown-recipes-from-the-whole-gang-2/ And keep reading for an excerpt of A Prince on the Run!

THANKS FOR TAKING THE time to read *Back to the Beginning*. If you enjoyed the story, would you consider taking a moment to leave a short review at the store where you bought it? I love to hear what readers think of my books. And honestly, word-of-mouth—via reviews—helps others in deciding whether to give books by indie authors like me a chance.

Thanks again,
Kristy

"Well, he isn't in a better mood today," Nolan muttered, rejoining Cameron on the deck. "I did get him to eat a little but it was like pulling teeth. I think I'd rather deal with an ornery bear."

"Do you think he'll ever-"

"Help! Can you help us please?"

"Oh dear God," Cameron gasped, whipping his head around to see Sam almost dragging his mother across the sand. She hung limply from his arms and it looked like the boy was quickly losing his hold on her.

Cameron knocked his chair over when he leaped up, and then he was running as fast as his feet would carry him. He heard Nolan yell at someone to get his bag, then footsteps pounding down the steps behind him, but he didn't look back to see who it was.

"Here, I've got her," Cameron told Sam, who was breathing so hard it almost sounded like he was sobbing. He relinquished the death grip he had on his mother, as Cameron swung her up into his arms and hurried toward the deck.

"What happened?" Nolan asked, grabbing her wrist and trying to find her pulse. No easy task as he jogged alongside them.

"She said she fell over some driftwood. Didn't know if she broke her ankle or sprained it. I tried to brace it, but I don't think it helped much. She fainted a few minutes ago." Cameron could hear the terror in his voice as he gently laid the woman on the chaise lounge.

"You did a good job with what you had available," Nolan assured him, quickly removing the makeshift brace and trying to look at the ankle. "She's going to need an x-ray, Cam. With the swelling and bruising, I can't even guess what's wrong with it. I do know I have to cut this pant leg away. It's cutting the circulation off. I need my bag!"

"Is she going to be okay?" Sam whispered. Cameron wrapped an arm around his shoulders in an attempt to comfort him.

"She's going to be just fine," Nolan said, taking the black bag Finley thrust at him. "What's her name?"

"Laura."

"Laura? Laura, can you hear me?" He waved a vial under her nose, causing her to choke a little. "Laura?"

"Y – yes?"

"I'm going to cut your jeans a little so we can release some of the pressure on your ankle. Hold very still please."

Cameron watched her wince as Nolan worked a pair of scissors between her ankle and the fabric and, though it didn't seem possible, her already chalky skin paled more. But she didn't make any noise, just glanced at her son and gave him what she probably thought was a reassuring smile. It didn't help. He could feel the boy was still trembling.

"We're going to have to get you down to the boat so we can get you to the mainland for an x-ray," Nolan explained, checking her pulse again.

"My jeep is parked at one of the piers in Mackinaw City."

"But the hospital is in St. Ignace," Finley said quietly, surprising Cameron. "I've got a vehicle at the pier there. And since you can't drive, we might as well just head there. Someone want to carry her to the boat? We'll take mine. It's faster."

"I'll carry her down," Cameron said quickly, brushing Nolan aside.

"But – my purse. My insurance card..."

"I'll get it, Mom. I'll be right back."

"Get a shirt, Sam," she called after him. Cameron chuckled. Once a mother, always a mother.

"Finley, can you grab a couple of pillows?" Nolan asked, tossing his things back in the bag. "We need to get that foot up."

"Your color is better," Cameron told her as he carried her down to the dock. "I'm glad, because your son was pretty worried."

"I can imagine," Laura murmured. "I'm really sorry to cause you all this trouble."

"It's no trouble. Don't worry about it." Her laugh was shaky.

"Right. No trouble. Uh-huh."

"Really, my only plans this morning were to try and read a book that I haven't been able to work up an interest in anyway, so you're not dragging me away from anything important. I'm just glad we were here and able to help." His laugh was a hair on the shaky side, too. "I'm especially glad that Nolan is a doctor and knows what to do."

"I'm still sorry. If I'd been paying more attention..." Her voice trailed off.

"Accidents are called accidents for a reason." Most of them anyway. Some were premeditated, and carefully planned, as he well knew. "Unless you do this kind of thing for fun, of course."

"Um- Fun? Let me think about that for a second." She appeared to consider his words thoughtfully, then slowly shook her head. "Nope. Zero fun."

Cameron burst out laughing. Many people in her situation would have trouble being pleasant, yet she seemed to find a little humor in it.

"It occurs to me that I don't even know your name," she said, as they stood on the dock waiting for the others.

"Cameron Rafferty at your service, ma'am."

"I'm Laura Keane."

"Pleased to meet you, Ms. Keane."

"Same here, Mr. Rafferty." She smiled at him, and Cameron felt his breath catch. "Mr. Rafferty-"

"Please. It's Cameron, or even Cam, if you prefer."

"Cameron, then. I know it's got to feel like I weigh about five hundred pounds by now. I think I'll be okay if you put me down."

"You're fine. They'll be here in a minute or two." She didn't weigh enough to be a bother. "See. Here comes Sam, and there's Nolan and Finley not far behind him."

Cameron passed Laura off to Finley after he jumped into the boat. For a man who wanted nothing to do with their neighbors the day before, he was surprisingly gentle as he placed Laura on the longest seat. From resenting their very presence, to this kindly solicitousness, it was really quite annoying.

"Let's get that foot up, Laura." Nolan handed her a Coke. "Drink some of this. You could use the sugar." He turned and handed one to Sam. "You could, too. Best medicine in the world," he said with a grin. "Go ahead and sit up front with Fin. We'll stay back here with your mom. Cam, we didn't bring enough pillows. You sit there. I'll take her feet."

Laura blushed as they made her, and themselves, as comfortable as possible. Cameron turned sideways in the corner so she could recline against his chest, and Nolan stacked the pillows on his lap, carefully placing her legs on top.

"Fin, I think we need to slow it down a bit. The water's pretty choppy today." Nolan had to shout to be heard over the motor and wind less than a minute into their trip. Cameron, too, had noticed that whatever color Laura had gotten back, quickly disappeared as the boat bucked and rocked over the whitecaps. "Have you ever used crutches before, Laura?"

"Crutches?" She looked a bit confused. "No."

"There's a secret to using them that most people aren't aware of," Nolan said with a cheerful smile, trying to take her mind off the pain, Cameron was sure.

"A secret?"

"Yes. Most people support their weight with their underarms, which makes their shoulders and back hurt more than they have to. Now trust me on this, you'll be using them for at least two weeks, depending on whether the ankle is broken or sprained. If you use them like that, you'll be sorry."

"So what other way is there to use them?"

"You keep your elbows stiff when you're walking. That way you use your arm strength, in addition to your hands and shoulders. It distributes the stress more evenly."

"Oh. That's a good idea," Laura agreed, keeping up a brave front. But Cameron could tell by the sound of her voice that the pain was worse again. Bouncing over some good-sized waves couldn't be helping at all.

"The doctor at the hospital is going to tell you to elevate your leg for most of the day for up to a week. It's important that you follow those instructions. Once the swelling goes down, I'll come over and show you some exercises to help things heal up in there."

On and on the distractions went, until they were piling in the big SUV Finley had rented. And finally it was just Finley, Sam, and Cameron in the waiting room. Nolan had insisted on accompanying Laura, which seemed to make both her and her son feel better. Cameron was dismayed to find that he wasn't relieved. He would have liked to have gone back with her too. Just to make sure everything was all right.

"Do you think she's going to be okay?" Sam asked, stopping his relentless pacing long enough to look at Cameron.

"Of course she is."

"She looked really sick."

"Pain can do that to anyone, Sam," Finley assured him, his voice gentle. "Once she's back home and not being jostled around all over the place, she'll be fine."

"I hope so. My- My dad died four years ago. She's all I have." Cameron wanted to hug the kid. He'd watched as Sam tried to act so grown up the day before, but this morning he was just a boy afraid of losing his mother.

"She'll be just fine," he promised. "You'll have to help her for a while though. Your mom strikes me as a pretty stubborn lady, so you'll have to make sure she doesn't overdo things." Sam chuckled.

"Stubborn? That's for sure. But I'll see to it that she rests. She won't be able to do anything but write."

"Your mom writes?" Cameron asked, surprised.

"Yes. Ever heard of Anna Laura Jacobs?"

"Can't say that I have."

"Well, I guess you wouldn't. She writes mystery romances. Most guys don't read that stuff. But she's good. She's won a bunch of awards."

"I'm impressed." Cameron watched as Sam got quiet, his gaze going back down the hall. When he looked back, he said,

"They're taking a long time with her, aren't they?"

So much for a distraction. He was back to pacing, an occasional growl coming from his stomach. Cameron guessed he hadn't had time for breakfast. Poor kid.

About the author...

KRISTY K. JAMES'S FIRST goal in life was to work in law enforcement, until the night she called the police to check out a scary noise in her yard. Realizing that she might someday have to check out scary noises in other dark yards if she continued on that path, she turned to her other favorite love... writing. Since then, her days have been filled with being a mom and reluctant zookeeper, creating stories and looking for trouble in her kitchen.

Connect with Kristy...

http://kristykjames.net/
https://www.facebook.com/kristykjames
Be sure to follow Kristy on Bookbub to get notifications for her new releases!
https://www.bookbub.com/authors/kristy-k-james
Other Works by Kristy K. James
Coach's Boys Series
The Daddy Pact, Book 1[1]
A Hero for Holly, Book 2[2]
A Harry Situation, Book 3[3]
Her Best Friend Jon, Book 4[4]
Code Red Christmas, Book 5[5]
Darby's Dilemma, Book 6[6]
The Detective's Second Chance, Book 7[7]
Back to the Beginning, Book 8[8]
Holding Out For Love, Coach's Boys Companion Story[9] (*should be read between books 6 & 7*)

---

1. http://kristykjames.net/books/the-daddy-pact/

2. http://kristykjames.net/books/a-hero-for-holly/

3. http://kristykjames.net/books/a-harry-situation/

4. http://kristykjames.net/books/her-best-friend-jon/

5. http://kristykjames.net/books/code-red-christmas/

6. http://kristykjames.net/books/darbys-dilemma/

7. http://kristykjames.net/books/the-detectives-second-chance/

8. http://kristykjames.net/books/10327/

9. http://kristykjames.net/books/holding-out-for-love/

<u>Cooking With the Coach's Boys</u>[10]

---

10. http://kristykjames.net/books/

cooking-with-the-coachs-boys-hometown-recipes-from-the-whole-gang-2/

A Royal Sweethearts Romance Novel Series

The Casteloria Royals

<u>A Prince on the Run, Book 1</u>[1]
<u>The Physician to the King, Book 2</u>[2]
<u>The Princess and the Bodyguard, Book 3</u>[3]

---

1. http://kristykjames.net/books/a-prince-on-the-run/

2. http://kristykjames.net/books/a-cool-summer-in-paradise/

3. http://kristykjames.net/books/a-cold-day-in-paradise/

Hemisphere/Paranormal Romance

The Ripple[1]

1. http://kristykjames.net/books/the-ripple/

Haunted Depot: The Ghost Curse Series

<u>The Secret, Book 1</u>[1]
<u>The Depot, Book 2</u>[2]
<u>A Merry Depot Christmas, Book 3</u>[3]

---

1. http://kristykjames.net/books/the-depot/

2. http://kristykjames.net/books/the-depot/

3. http://kristykjames.net/books/a-merry-depot-christmas/

Special Wishes Time Travel Romance

His Only Love[1]
Her Long Road Home[2]

---

1. http://kristykjames.net/books/holding-on-to-yesterday/

2. http://kristykjames.net/books/the-accidental-wish/

Other Fiction:

Enza[1]
Josh[2]
The Secret Admirer[3]
Erin's Christmas Wish[4]
A Fine Mess[5]
Reluctant Guardian[6]

---

1. http://kristykjames.net/books/enza/

2. http://kristykjames.net/books/josh/

3. http://kristykjames.net/books/the-secret-admirer/

4. http://kristykjames.net/books/erins-christmas-wish/

5. http://kristykjames.net/books/a-fine-mess/

6. http://kristykjames.net/books/reluctant-guardian/